KATE on the CASE

HANNAH PECK

PICCADILLY
PRESS

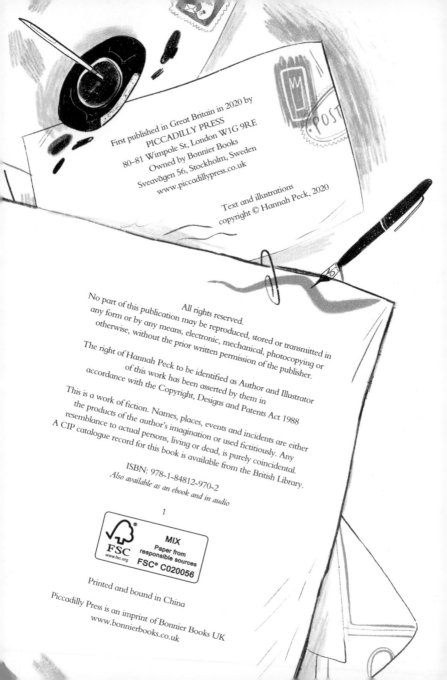

First published in Great Britain in 2020 by
PICCADILLY PRESS
80–81 Wimpole St, London W1G 9RE
Owned by Bonnier Books
Sveavägen 56, Stockholm, Sweden
www.piccadillypress.co.uk

Text and illustrations
copyright © Hannah Peck, 2020

This is a work of fiction. Names, places, events and incidents are either
the products of the author's imagination or used fictitiously. Any
resemblance to actual persons, living or dead, is purely coincidental.

A CIP catalogue record for this book is available from the British Library.

ISBN: 978-1-84812-970-2
Also available as an ebook and in audio

MIX
Paper from
responsible sources
FSC® C020056
www.fsc.org

Printed and bound in China

Piccadilly Press is an imprint of Bonnier Books UK
www.bonnierbooks.co.uk

Please return/ renew this item
by the last date shown.
Books can also be renewed at
www.bolton.gov.uk/libraries

KATE

OUR MAIN CHARACTER
& ASPIRING SPECIAL CORRESPONDENT

SPECIAL
CORRESPONDANT
MANUAL

QUIET SHOES
FOR SNEAKING

& RUPERT : BEST FRIEND. DELIVERER OF
RALLYING SPEECHES. A MOUSE.

The Kitchen

The CONSERVATORY

LIBRARY   LUGGAGE

WELCOME ABOARD!
FOR ANY QUERIES YOU MAY HAVE,
ASK A FELLOW PASSENGER, OR CONSULT
THE LIBRARY. ENJOY THE JOURNEY!
— SIMON
(CONDUCTOR-IN-TRAINING)

CHAPTER ONE

Kate was ready to board the train. Her
bag was packed with enough clothes
for the week-long trip, her *Special
Correspondent Manual* was clasped in
her hands, and Rupert, her pet mouse,
was nestled in the top pocket of her red
coat.

'Hurry up, Kate!' Dad pushed through
the crowd with his enormous shoulders
and began shooing her towards the train's

metal steps. 'If we miss this one, we won't see Mum for another week!'

Kate's mum was a scientist and was on the brink of a Very Exciting Discovery involving Arctic seaweed. Kate had received a letter from her the day before. It was still crisped up with cold when it dropped through the letter box, and it said:

Kate, I.P.A. APPROVED

I can't wait to see you next week. The longest conversation I've had all month was with a nomadic seal — a PARTICULARLY one-sided affair. Bring some proper food with you too, won't you? I can't stomach noodled eels for much longer. (YUCK).

Mum x

Because Mum couldn't leave her post, the International Polar Association had sent Kate and her dad a ticket to visit. The only way to get there was by the steam train, which was almost ready to leave. It was old but shiny, and painted a brilliant blue.

Kate was just about to step on board when two golden eyes flashed in the black gap beneath the carriage. She blinked, and they vanished.

'Did you see that, Roo?' Kate whispered into her pocket.

Rupert squeaked in a way that meant, 'Yes – and I'm not sure I liked it . . .'

Before either of them could think, they were bundled up the steps by Dad and plopped on the polished wooden floor.

'Now, stay in this carriage, my sweets – I'll go and find our compartment.'

The train was even fancier on the inside than it was on the outside. Gold candleholders and velvet lampshades stood on dark wooden tables, alongside little silver bells with labels like 'Ring me for orange juice' and 'I'd like earplugs, please'.

Even the cushions are frilly! thought Kate, climbing onto an armchair and lowering her bottom onto the biggest, fluffiest one.

Only it wasn't a cushion at all.

It was a cat. A very angry cat that arched its back, spread its daggery claws, and sprang straight at Kate and Rupert.

Fortunately the cat rather overestimated his airborne skills and landed with a furry thud on the floor.

'See, Roo?' said Kate, once she had stopped laughing, 'The eyes we saw under the train probably belonged to this puffy old thing.'

'Excuse me,' hissed a voice from behind them. Kate spun round to see an old lady as thin as a weasel, holding a pointy cane with an enormous diamond on top.

'*That puffy old thing* is named Master Mimkins. An apology, please!'

'That's his name?!' Rupert squeaked, causing

a brand-new set of giggles that were impossible to stifle.

The weasel-lady's eyes narrowed. 'Master Mimkins The Third is one hundred and twenty per cent pure pedigree – he's the last of his kind!'

Kate looked at Master Mimkins, who had just stuffed an entire paw into his mouth, causing his eyes to cross in the process.

'No wonder he's the only one left,' she muttered to Rupert.

The lady had just opened her thin purple lips to continue telling them off when a skinny young man staggered onto the train carrying an enormous pile of luggage. He wore a blue and gold

uniform, on which a badge reading

was pinned.

'Pardon me, Madame Maude. Pardon me, child and mouse,' he honked. 'Luggage coming through!'

Everyone shuffled out of the way. Everyone except – yes, really – Master Mimkins, who was frowning at his own reflection in a vase.

Kate would later write in her diary that what happened next was 'Total and Utter Chaos'.

Simon stepped directly on Master Mimkins's tail. Master Mimkins

let out a terrible shrieking
'YEEEEEOOOOOOOWW!'

Luggage toppled everywhere.

Pants whizzed past Kate's nose
and caught on a candelabra.
False teeth chattered
under tables. A jar of
pickled eggs bounced
away down the aisle.
A whole stack of golden
trophies clattered out of
a small red case and
landed at Madame
Maude's feet.

Amidst all the confusion, Kate saw a glimmer in Madame Maude's magpie eyes.

'I'm s-s-so sorry,' stammered Simon, his long legs flailing as he scrabbled around on the floor, stuffing everything back into random suitcases. He grabbed the jar of eggs and stood up, but – *CRACK* – collided directly with Madame Maude's pointy diamond cane, soaking her in egg juice.

Silence.

She stood as still as a statue, eggy water running off her clothes. She stared long and hard at Kate, before spinning round with a swish of her long coat and stalking off up the corridor, a bristling Master Mimkins at her heels.

'I don't like that lady,' said Kate, getting down on her hands and knees to help Simon gather up all the spilled belongings.

'Madame Maude,' said Simon, who was still as red as a sunburned tomato, 'is our most prestigious guest aboard. Apparently she used to be quite famous.'

'For what?' said Rupert. 'Being rich and rude?'

'She's more than just rude,' muttered Kate. 'Under the smell of eggs I'm sure I caught a whiff of something fishy.'

CHAPTER TWO

Kate didn't like Madame Maude, but she wasn't going to stay annoyed when there was a whole train to explore and, no doubt, many hidden stories for a Special Correspondent to report.

Together she and Rupert found a small library stuffed with old books – where they met a pensive Russian priest conversing with a bored-looking man called Mr Billie, a conservatory – where a glass ceiling revealed the fading pink of a winter sky, an impressive dining car and, just beyond that, a kitchen.

Peering round the silver door they found Simon the Conductor-in-Training leaning over a vat of bubbling beige goo and peering at a recipe book, a wooden spoon in one hand and a dishcloth in the other.

'A pinch of salt?' he was muttering to himself. 'A *pinch*? What is this – a riddle?'

'Shouldn't you be conducting the train?' Kate asked nervously, making him jump.

'Kate! The kitchen is

ABSOLUTELY
Out of Bounds for
children and small
animals.' He flapped
a dirty dishcloth at them.
'There are knives galore!
Off you go!'

'I'm not looking forward
to breakfast, if that's what
we're getting,' said Rupert
as they scurried back down
the train, pockets full of
emergency bread rolls
stolen for this very reason.

They spent the rest
of the evening settling
into a small but cosy

compartment with Dad. While he fussed about, unpacking and lining up his aftershave bottles in order of 'what smell suits what time of day', Kate laid out Roo's special sleeping sock on her pillow.

It was at breakfast the next day that the drama began. Everyone was in the dining car, trying not to slop their breakfast of runny scrambled egg (a vast improvement on the mess Kate had seen behind the scenes) down their fronts, when a high-pitched voice cut through the chatter.

It was Miss Bonbon, a very elegant passenger who wore a lot of scarves. They had shared a lovely chat about adventures

the previous evening, but now she was looking sad, and standing at the door in her dressing gown. 'They've all g-g-gone!' she stammered. 'My gymnastics trophies! All sixteen of them!' The carriage erupted into 'What?'s and 'Goodness me!'s and a couple of simultaneous 'Is there anything she can't do?!'s from a pair of twins with vivid red plaits.

Only Madame Maude remained silent, sipping on her boiling water, Master Mimkins curled on her lap.

'I hate to break even more bad news,' said Simon the Conductor-in-Training over the murmurs, 'but the trophies aren't the only things that are missing.'

A collective hush fell over the breakfasters.

'Three packets of Extremely Flavoursome Ginger-Nut Biscuits have gone from under my bunk,' he whispered dramatically.

There was more silence.

'That's nothing, you twit!' said Chloe from the back of the car.

'Ginger-nut biscuits are disgusting!' said Zoe. 'You have terrible taste in biscuits!'

'QUIET!'

bellowed a man's voice. Dad was standing on his chair, looking even larger than usual. Everyone fell silent and looked at him.

'We can squabble about biscuits till our scrambled eggs

solidify on our plates – and wouldn't that be a sorry way to start the day? – *or* we can talk this through sensibly. Let's not get ahead of ourselves and turn this train into a crime scene just yet. I'm sure there's an explanation.'

'There's hope for my biscuits yet!' gulped Simon through tears of gratitude.

'Fine,' muttered everyone else.

'But what about my trophies?' Miss Bonbon was still flushed. 'I'm not Bonbon the Brilliant and Back-Springing Beam Queen without them!'

'We'll organise a search,' said Kate's dad, getting down from his chair. 'After all, they must be here somewhere. In the meantime, let's all try to remain calm.'

People gradually went back to their breakfasts, but the atmosphere felt a little more chilly than it had before – and Kate didn't think it had anything to do with the wisps of snow that had started falling outside.

'We saw those trophies yesterday when Simon dropped all that luggage,' she whispered to Rupert, who was sitting in an empty teacup. 'And Madame Maude *looked* at them, Roo!'

'You can't blame her just for looking at them,' he said through a mouthful of toast. 'I looked at them too.'

'But it was the *way* she looked at them! She was practically licking her lips.'

'But she's got a giant diamond! It's not

like she needs any more stuff, is it?'

'Ah, Rupert,' Kate said sagely, 'didn't you hear the Russian priest last night? The only thing riches do is make you want more of them.'

'That's easy for *him* to say,' muttered Rupert.

But Kate wasn't listening. It was time to consult *The Special Correspondent Manual*. If anyone knew how to proceed,

it was the author, her One True Idol, Catherine Rodríguez.

Kate decided in that single moment that she was going to solve this mystery. Madame Maude's lips were sure to be as tightly sealed as a jar of gherkins, but that wouldn't stop Kate from questioning everyone else she could.

COULD I PULL OFF A SUIT? PROBABLY NOT...

First you must decide what exactly you are reporting on, and why it is important. In my early career, fresh out of Newspaper School, I wrote many stories that were important to me, but not so much everyone else (See 'A Not So Brief History of Khakis'). Your story should be necessary and relevant to your readers, revealing information that is crucial to them. So, let us begin with some starting points:

YES!

- Are strange things happening?

- Is someone acting suspiciously?

- Do you have reason to believe the truth is being compromised?

After you have answered these questions, you must find your way in. An excellent technique is INTERVIEWS.

→ in funk?

HOW TO CONDUCT AN INTERVIEW

The best reports include other people's stories too.
You never know what new and interesting perspective
they may lend, or what vital clues they are privy to.

Provide a calm setting for your interview. This may
include biscuits.

Start with small talk to put your interviewee at ease
– this will often lead to more interesting topics.
Don't be afraid of silences. You can simply nod.
Write everything down.

TIPS FOR REMAINING PROFESSIONAL

Make sure you have eaten well. An empty
stomach equals poor judgement.

WORK ON SPELLING

Use pencil, not a pen. You can make mistakes
just like everybody else.

Catherine Rodríguez

CHAPTER THREE

By eleven thirty-six that morning, Kate's bunk was no longer a bunk. It was a detective booth.

First to be questioned were the twins from Compartment No. 6: Chloe and Zoe. Their bright red plaits were so long they could sit on them, but right now they were chewing on the ends nervously.

'We were both in our compartment last night,' said Zoe.

'Yes,' said Chloe.

'What were you doing?' asked Kate.

'Nothing, really.'

'Nothing at all?' asked Kate.

'No,' said Chloe. 'I mean . . . Yes.'

'You just said "No", Chloe,' said Kate, who was beginning to suspect she might be looking forward to an illustrious career in detective work.

'Yes,' said Chloe.

'No, she didn't,' said Zoe. She poked Chloe with the wet end of her plait.

'Oh, we might as well just tell her,' sighed Chloe.

'Fine,' said Zoe. 'Although you have to promise not to tell anyone, Kate.'

Kate solemnly placed her hand on *The*

Special Correspondent Manual. 'You have my word.'

'We're running away to join the circus,' said Chloe coolly. 'I know it's a cliché, but what else are we supposed to do? It's not as if there is a circus at home in the Hebrides. Last night we were practising our routine.'

'I see,' said Kate, secretly very impressed. 'And do you need anything for this routine? Trophies to prove you're Hebridean champions? Biscuits for . . . um . . . sustenance?'

'Nope, the only thing we've ever stolen are utensils from Granny's kitchen,' said Zoe. 'We experimented with a bit of knife juggling, but Chloe got annoyed when her finger was chopped off.'

'What can I say?' Chloe shrugged.
'I can be dramatic. Now our act is mainly plait-oriented. Skipping, lassoing, performative crocheting – that sort of thing.'

'I see,' said Kate again, nodding as if she was very In The Know with circus talk.

There was no motive here, she thought gloomily, pencilling a giant red X next to Rupert's drawing of the twins, before seeing them out.

Next was Simon the Conductor-in-Training.

'How long have you been training for, Simon?'

'Three years, six months and forty-five

days,' he replied cheerfully.

'That's a long time to be in training . . .' Kate said.

Simon shrugged. 'Well, I'm doing the best I can – and there's a lot that needs to be done around here, you know.'

Kate thought back to Simon's cooking

and silently agreed. But back to business.
It was time to turn up the heat.

'And what –' Kate lowered her voice
for maximum impact – 'were you doing
last night at the time Miss Bonbon's
trophies went missing?'

'Reading.'

'A book isn't a very good alibi.'

'Oh, Kate, you're just so clever!'
interrupted a beaming Dad from the
corner of the compartment where he
was refolding their towels into origami
animals. 'Who would have thought you'd
grow into such a sophisticated –'

'Dad! I'm investigating!'

'Oops! Didn't mean to interrupt!'

Time for one last question.

'What were you reading?'

'*Trains: What They Are and How to Work Them*. It's been a real life-saver! Did you know this thing runs on steam?'

Last was the Russian priest. He had a kind face, and was keen to point out that stealing was a 'bit of a no-no' when you're a priest.

'Plus,' he admitted in a whisper, 'I'm gluten-free, so no ginger biscuits for me! Nothing clears out a congregation faster than a surprise visit from the unholy ghost!'

'What does he mean?' asked Rupert quietly.

'A fart, Rupert,' said Kate. 'He's talking about a fart.'

But just as he was about to leave, the priest turned back.

'You might find this useful,' he said vaguely. 'Something mildly suspicious happened to me this morning.'

Kate leaned in. 'Yes?'

'I woke to find my Ancient Scrolls were gone.'

'WHAT?' said Kate. Another theft!

'Why didn't you tell us sooner?'

'Earthly possessions aren't really top of my list,' said the priest. 'I've got them memorised, you see – although of course I have been praying for their imminent return.'

'This is huge, Rupert,' muttered Kate, scribbling as fast as she could manage. 'Was there anything at the scene of the crime?' she asked the priest.

'Nothing really,' said the priest. 'I probably bought them in on my slippers.'

'Bought what in?' said Kate.

'The whiskers.'

'That settles it, Roo,' said Kate as soon as they were alone again. 'Who do we know with whiskers?'

'Master Mimkins!' breathed Rupert.

'Exactly. *And* Madame Maude is refusing to be questioned. If that's not suspicious, I don't know what is. I think we're going to have to employ some serious sneakery.'

ChAPTER FOUR

It soon became apparent that getting inside Madame Maude's compartment was going to be a tricky business indeed. For starters, she didn't have a regular one like everybody else.

'Oh no!' Simon had said, when Kate had asked him. 'She's got the entirety of Suite No. 7 to herself.'

'This is rubbish, Roo,' said Kate. They were sitting outside on the tiny iron balcony at the end of the dining car, snow whizzing past their dangling feet. It was cold, but the only place they could talk properly without being overheard. 'How are we going to find out what Madame Maude and her cranky cat are up to?'

Kate dug *The Special Correspondent Manual* out of her coat, careful not to let any of the insides blow away in the icy wind. 'Let's see what our friend Catherine has to say about distractions . . .'

Using distractions to hunt down a tricky story is high-
level correspondenting. You might need to distract
someone for just a second while you slide an important
document out of their desk drawer and into your pocket,
or perhaps you require them to leave a room of Top
Secret and potentially scandalous archives unattended.

Either way, first you must decide what your
distraction will be. Here's how:

Who are you distracting?

MADAME MAUDE!!

What are they like?

EVIL, ANGRY, HIGHLY PRIVATE.

What are their interests?

CATS? jars of eggs

APPROVED

Oxford, England – 1997.

I used a mechanical 'babbling bilderwing' to engross naturalist C. A. Bloom, giving me time to photograph his poisonous invention (see Fig. 2).

Milan, Italy – 1967.

Glamorous targets of Operation 'Fancy' were so distracted by the height and decor of this specially made cake, they failed to notice a camera hidden inside the top layer.

OPERATION 'FANCY', 1967

'What's most valuable to Madame Maude?' mused Rupert. 'Anything she can get her hands on, by the look of things!'

'I've got it!' he squeaked. 'You've seen the way she fusses over Master Mimkins. I bet she'd follow him *anywhere.*'

'But how do we make Master Mimkins move? What are you sugges—'

'I'm a mouse,' said Rupert, 'and Master Mimkins is a cat.'

Kate looked at him. And then it dawned on her.

'Oh, Roo, you can't!' she breathed. 'We can't use *YOU* as a distraction!'

Rupert drew himself up to his full height, which was about half a centimetre taller than usual.

'I may be a small mouse, but I've got the heart of a really big one. And I've got more brains in the end of my tail than that cat's got in its whole lavender-shampooed head! I would take it as an insult to my intelligence if you thought Master mughead Mimkins could outsmart me!'

'He could never *outsmart* you, Roo,' said Kate, 'but he could *catch* you. Then what would I do?!'

But five minutes of a very persuasive mouse later, the pair were back inside their compartment, planning a scribbly but brilliantly foolproof plan.

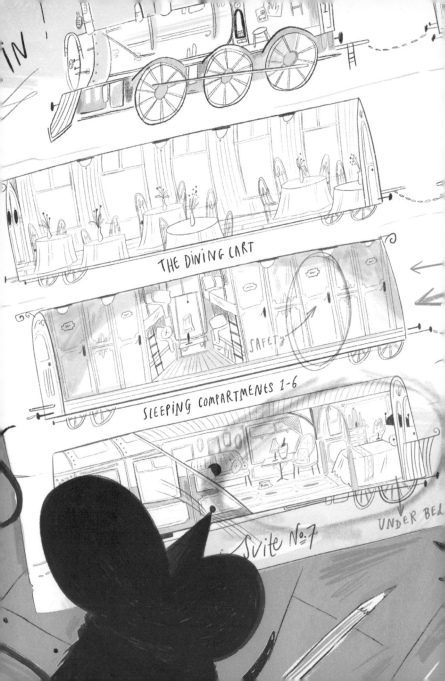

THE DIVING CART

SAFETY

SLEEPING COMPARTMENTES 1-6

Suite No.7

UNDER BED

The CONSERVAT
R. TO DIVE UNDER DOORS
- MM CAN'T.
LUGGAGE
LIBRARY
WELCOME ABOARD!
FOR ANY QUERIES YOU MAY HAVE,
CONSULT
FIND WHAT
SHE IS
HIDING!
!!
THE TROPHIES
GET
HERE

CHAPTER FIVE

Everything was in place. It was three
o'clock in the afternoon and the corridors
were clear. Kate and Roo walked as
casually as they could through the dining
car, the conservatory, the yards and yards
of long wooden hallways, and past the
luggage car – until they arrived.

The doors to Suite No. 7 was dark
wood, and looked shinier than the regular
ones everywhere else. Roo hopped out

of Kate's pocket and into her palm. She kissed him on the nose, then set him down on the floor, where he did a few quick star jumps, took one deep breath and slipped under the gap and into Madame Maude's private quarters.

Kate looked at the door, feeling a sudden pang of fear for tiny, brave Rupert and what was waiting for him on the other side. She squeezed into her hiding spot, behind a giant decorative urn, and not a moment too soon.

The door burst open, and a ball of fur shot out like a firework. Kate saw a flash of sharp teeth as it whipped past – Rupert's plan had better work!

Kate waited for Madame Maude to come sprinting after him . . .

but no one appeared.

And then it dawned on her.

Of course! Madame Maude

wouldn't
sprint! Even
a brisk jog was
completely beneath her.

Kate's heart beat faster – she had to
do something! But what? She peered into
Madame Maude's huge compartment
and saw her lying on the bed with slices
of pickled gherkins on her eyes. That is
categorically yuck, thought Kate. And
hadn't she noticed that Master Mimkins
was gone?

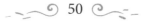

Kate thought fast – what would Catherine Rodríguez do? Kate pinched her cheeks till they were pink and then burst into the carriage.

'M-Madame Maude,' she panted, as if she had run the whole length of the train.

'Is that you, Simon? Fetch me my slippers, will you? And not the white ones – you know how they irritate my bunions.'

'N-no, it's me, Kate!'

Silence.

'Master Mimkins has gone totally bananas – he's chasing my mouse!'

Madame Maude yawned. 'Good for him.'

Kate went red for real this time — how dare she!

'And he's eaten an entire pyramid of chocolate eggs!'

'That CAAAT!' Madame Maude swiped the gherkins from her face and leaped to her bunion-y feet.

'He's going to be

And with that she finally left the carriage — albeit it in her usual mincing

walk rather than the pacy stride Kate had
hoped for.

CHAPTER SIX

Madame Maude's carriage was like a life-sized jewellery box. Everything was plush and glittering, and the *clickety-clack* of the train was muffled by thick lavender carpets and heavy curtains.

There was no time to lose. Kate knew there were three places where people hide their secret things. Number one: under the bed. But no, there was nothing there but a few empty cans of Fishy-Delishy.

Number two was the underwear drawer, but again, nothing there other than a few pairs of pants.

I wonder why they're so tattered, thought Kate. It's not like she can't afford new knickers . . .

The third place people hide things: in plain sight. Kate looked around the room. It was so obvious! On the top of the dresser was a silver box. Kate crept closer. It was old and unpolished, but she could make out two whisks shaped like an X engraved on the top.

Kate lifted the lid, her heart in her mouth. She was

certain she was about
to discover Something
Very Important. Inside lay
a stack of old yellowing
papers.

Newspaper clippings!
But there was no time
to read them now.
She quickly stuffed
the box down
her jumper and
ran out of the
carriage, fast.

The corridors were quiet and empty. Where was Rupert? Kate hurried through the luggage car, past the sleeping compartments and into the conservatory. Dad was snoozing in an armchair. The twins were playing an aggressively silent game of Scrabble. Miss Bonbon was reading *Hobbies for High-Functioning Adrenaline-Seekers*. And there was no sign of Master Mimkins, Madame Maude or – gulp – Rupert.

'Psssst! Up here!'

Kate's heart leaped. 'Roo?'

He was perched high up on a curtain pole, but slid down the velvet fabric with a *whoosh*, straight into Kate's open hands.

'What happened? Why is everything so calm?'

'It turns out Master Mimkins can't tell the difference between a real mouse and the reflection of one. He thought I was hiding inside an urn and dived straight into it!'

'Brilliant!' Kate snorted. 'Where's Madame Maude?'

'She's with Simon, making him
squeeze Master Mimkins out. Anyway,
what did you find?'

'I'm not entirely sure,' Kate replied.
'All I know is we've got some reading to
do.'

THE TRIPLE TRIFLE RECIPE BROUGHT TO YOU BY NEWLY APPOINTED GOLDEN WHISK JUDGE—

CAN WE HAVE MAUDE?
PLEASE SIR, CAN WE HAVE SOME

1oz CREAM
2cups BURNT OR 1cup BUTTERMILK
½lb BRAZIL NUTS, ch
½lb CANDIED PINEAPP

MA'AM WITH A NAAN — Maude in India!

A CAREER AS GOLDEN AS HER TROPHIES. MAUDE
BEEN INSTRUMENTAL IN DISCOVERING MANY TA
CHEFS FROM ALL OVER THE WORLD, TRAINING THE
INSPIRING CULINARY
ARTISTRY.

FOR YEARS, B

The Lookout Post

60/79

APPLAUDE FOR MAUDE

MADAME MAUDE WINS GOLDEN
WHISK COOKING CHAMPIONSHIP.

"I FEEL HONOURED"

WIN a trip to the GW test Kitchen!

IT ALL STARTED
WITH AN OYSTER...

SPLITS

WHISKED AWAY!
MAUDE STRIPPED OF PRIZE.

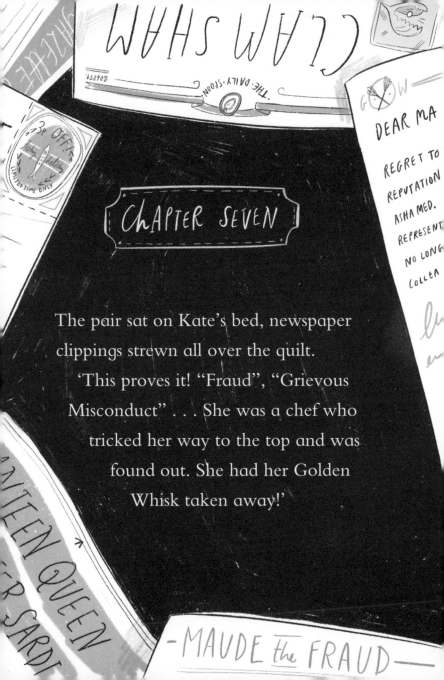

CLAM SHAM

· THE·DAILY·SPOON ·

DEAR MA

REGRET TO
REPUTATION
ASHAMED.
REPRESENT
NO LONG
COLLEA

CHAPTER SEVEN

The pair sat on Kate's bed, newspaper
clippings strewn all over the quilt.

'This proves it! "Fraud", "Grievous
Misconduct" . . . She was a chef who
tricked her way to the top and was
found out. She had her Golden
Whisk taken away!'

QUEEN

SARDI

— MAUDE the FRAUD —

'What's all this about oysters?' asked Rupert.

Kate scanned the paper nearest her. 'So apparently she lied to the judging panel about what type of oysters she was using for a top-secret dish. What a cheat!'

'Why would she want to keep all these though?' Rupert gestured at the incriminating articles surrounding them.

'I'm not sure . . . Maybe she's plotting revenge, or wants to remind herself not to make the same mistakes, or –'

'Hang on,' interrupted Rupert, who was sifting through the papers with his tiny paws, 'there's something else in here!'

Unlike the rest, this piece of paper was crisp and white. It had big red letters at the top.

FINAL NOTICE

DEAR MADAME MAUDE,

AFTER OBLIGING YOUR REQUEST TO 'LOOK HARDER', WE REGRET TO INFORM YOU THERE IS <u>UNDOUBTEDLY NO MONEY</u> LEFT IN YOUR ACCOUNT. UNLESS YOU CAN REPAY YOUR DEBTS, WE WILL BE TERMINATING YOUR CONTRACT WITH US.

WE, HOWEVER, WILL REMAIN-CORDIALLY-

THE BANK   Sig: The Bank

PS: WE ARE ALSO REPOSSESSING YOUR HOUSE.

For one second Kate felt sorry for
Madame Maude. Then she remembered
how suspicious and pointy and angry she
was, and everything fell into place.

'Do you think this is why she's been stealing from everyone on board? Because she's run out of money?'

'Gymnastics trophies are probably worth millions!' agreed Rupert.

'And what about Simon's Extremely Flavoursome Ginger-Nut Biscuits?' mused Kate.

'She probably got hungry – being a thief must be tiring work!'

It was all coming together. Kate could practically see the proud look on Catherine Rodríguez's face. Perhaps her findings could make their way into a newspaper themselves! But before Kate could get too carried away, there was a murmur on the other side of the compartment door. It grew to a scuffle, which grew to a mass of voices, which grew to –

'A commotion!' exclaimed Kate, rushing to the door. 'I bet something else has gone missing!'

They slipped out of their compartment – and were nearly knocked over by a stampede of people. People with looks of total fear on their faces.

CHAPTER EIGHT

'I'm going to be eaten!' cried the usually very quiet and private Mr Billie as he ran past, arms in the air.

'Look at me – I'm

UNQUESTIONABLY
DELICIOUS!'

'Just let him try!' shouted Miss Bonbon, sprinting after him as she pushed the sleeves of her dress up to her shoulders. 'I've wrestled crocodiles in Argentina wearing nothing but a leaf!'

'Why is everyone panicking?' Kate yelled over the frenzy. 'DAD?!'

She started weaving through legs, but in her hurry bumped straight into Simon.

'It's bitten me! It's got me!' he shrieked. 'I'll die never knowing who stole my biscuits!'

'It's just me!' insisted Kate. 'What's going on?'

'T-t-tiger!' he stammered. 'I saw it just now! In the kitchen! Mouth wide open, ready to eat me!'

'My uncle had his arm bitten clean off at the zoo!' yelled someone. 'Tigers love eating arms!'

'The fingers especially!' shouted another. 'They're like picnic sausages to

tigers! Once they
start eating them, it is
literally impossible for
them to stop!'

'A *tiger*?' scoffed Kate to Rupert, who
was looking just as confused as Kate felt.
'On this train? That's just ridiculous!'

But Simon replied in utter seriousness
when the twins, their eyes as wide
as ping-pong balls, asked him what
happened next. 'I ran away, of course!
Sped out of there before the beast could
get a taste of all this!' He gestured at his
lanky limbs with pride.

'I think,' said Madame Maude, quietly
from the end of the corridor, 'that safety
has to be the top priority. We need to stay

out of harm's way. I propose a curfew.'

The crowd fell silent.

'Everyone is to stay in their own compartments from half past six in the evening to eight o'clock in the morning. If there really is a tiger on board, that's when it'll be roaming.'

For a split second Kate thought that Madame Maude looked at her directly when she said this.

'Good idea, Maude,' Dad said with a nod. He had made his way to the middle of the anxious crowd. 'It's probably best to leave your trophy search for later, Miss Bonbon. It doesn't seem sensible to go poking around, not after what Simon's just seen.'

The crowd dispersed, muttering their theories as to how a tiger might have come to be on the train, and how exactly he was planning to eat them.

'Everyone on this train is going bananas!' said Kate, once they had all cleared off. 'First a thief, and now a tiger!'

'Do you think he's telling the truth?' Rupert squeaked. 'That there's an actual tiger on the train?'

'Of course there

isn't,' Kate replied. 'Can't you see, Rupert? It's all Madame Maude! She's got Simon under her thumb, and with everyone obeying her curfew, she can do whatever she wants. Well, she might have fooled everyone else, but not us. She must think we're as stupid as Master Mimkins looks when he's eating his dinner . . .'

CHAPTER NINE

'Now, darling,' said Dad, 'you know I am very much impressed with your dedication to Special Correspondenting, but tonight I want you tucked up safe with Roo.'

It was getting dark outside. After a slightly cold dinner, everyone had hurried off to their compartments under the new curfew. Trees made spiky black shapes against the low-hanging moon as they sped past.

'The last thing I want is for you to meet your mother with an arm missing. Or missing altogether.'

He began locking the door with multiple padlocks.

'Why are you locking all the locks?' Kate asked.

'Because of the tiger, sweetie!

We don't want a surprise visitor tonight!
Nor do I want you investigating
anything, I'm afraid.'

Kate's stomach sank. With the
corridors free and everyone locked
away, Madame Maude could get up to
whatever sneaky business she wanted.
And Kate wasn't going to let her.

But how was she going to get out of
the compartment? The bunch of keys was
now firmly lodged under Dad's pillow,
which would soon be under his sleeping
head.

Kate waited until Dad's earplugs were
in and his eyes were shut before switching
on her torch and opening up *The Special*

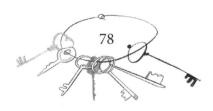

Correspondent Manual. She looked at the tattered photograph of Catherine Rodríguez, her One True Idol. What would she do in this *situation*?

Wait until morning? No, Catherine Rodríguez would most certainly *not* sit

around in a bunk bed while there was a
story unfolding just beyond her door.

'This is impossible, Rupert,' said Kate.
'Perhaps I should just go to sleep and
forget all about this mess.'

Rupert made a noise Kate had never
heard before. It was somewhere between
a squeak and a *pffft*. He climbed onto
her pillow, stood up on his
little pink legs and puffed
out his tiny chest.

'You are absolutely

Not

going to sit
around here

and do nothing,' he peeped. 'You're Kate! Special Correspondent! Daughter of one of the most successful Arctic explorers in the world! If you don't find a way out of here and solve this mystery, I'll do it myself!'

Suddenly Dad sat up straight in his bed. Kate switched off the torch and froze. Had they woken him? 'My wife . . .' he mumbled, 'the cleverest of all of the seaweeds . . .' before collapsing back down into his cosy blankets with a giant snore.

'That was close,' whispered Kate grimly. 'Let's get those keys.'

CHAPTER TEN

Extracting the keys wasn't the hard part.
It was looking at Dad's sleeping face
while she slipped them out from their
hiding place. Kate hoped she would be
able to tell him everything, and soon.

Click CLACK Rattle
CREEEEEEAAK

And then they were out. Armed with
her trusty torch and a can of Fishy-
Delishy – for who knew when they might
need to distract an angry Master Mimkins
– Kate and Rupert crept through the
empty train.

At first every moonlit lampshade
was a thieving Madame Maude, every
embroidered cushion her glowing white

cat. But it soon
became clear that neither of
them was striding up and down the
corridors, nor was Madame Maude

gleefully helping herself to the contents of
the luggage car.

'The kitchen,' Rupert breathed after
they had successfully sneaked through
the conservatory and into
the dining car.

'That's where she doesn't want us. I bet that's where we'll find her, or her stash of stolen goods . . .'

'Of course!' Kate whispered back. 'You saw the way Simon panicked when we slipped in the other day – and it *just so happens* this is where the supposed "tiger" is hiding out. What a load of dirty pants.'

They were close now – the door to the kitchen car was just ahead.

Was it just Kate's imagination, or was this carriage darker than the others? The moon appeared to have vanished altogether, so that it seemed as if Kate's torch was the only light in the world.

She opened the door and stepped inside.

All of a sudden there was a whip of cold air. Kate dropped the torch, plunging them into blackness.

Then there were two eyes. Two gleaming eyes. Two gleaming eyes like apricots. And they were looking straight at Kate.

Kate was frozen to the spot. She wanted to run, but her legs wouldn't work. All she could do was listen as a velvet voice issued from the dark, looping around her like smoke.

'You think "Fishy-Delishy" will tempt
  me out?
Back here there's brie and sauerkraut.
You'll have to do much better, girl,
Than smelly scraps of spotted trout.'

Kate could feel Roo's little heart beating
fast against her own. This most certainly
wasn't the voice of Master Mimkins.

'W-who are you?' stammered Kate.
No answer. Then . . .

WHOOOOOO OOOOSHH!

The gas rings were lit all at once, and the kitchen was thrown into a blue and orange whirl of light. Standing in front of them, silhouetted against the flames . . .

Was . . .

A . . .

Tiger.

CHAPTER ELEVEN

He was enormous. Up-to-the-ceiling, arms-the-size-of-six-year-old-children enormous. The type of enormous that was the last thing people saw before they were eaten and their bones spat out like toothpicks.

He was wearing an apron splattered with red. A hat like a giant sinister meringue was perched upon his head.

Rupert let out a high-pitched scream. Kate was flooded with panic. What did this all mean?

And – more importantly – was she about to be eaten?!

'STOP!'

she cried. 'I probably taste horrible! I'm not made of sugar and spice and all things nice; I probably taste like notebooks and pencils!'

The Tiger laughed a slow, silky laugh.

Kate noticed his teeth, which were perfectly white and very, very sharp. *'You think that I would want to eat YOU? By the stripes on my back, you're no tiramisu!'* 'What?' Kate was confounded. 'Well, what's all this then?' She glanced around at the lit stove, the red-splashed apron, the rows of knives on the countertops. 'And w-w-why

are you speaking in
rhyming couplets?'
stammered Rupert.
   '*Firstly,*' snapped the Tiger,
     'I don't know what you mean.
To constantly rhyme?
     What a tiresome routine.'
   He paused and sighed
a long, dramatic sigh.
   'But I suppose it's about
       time I told my story,
My struggle . . .
     my rise . . .
     my fall from
     glory.'

'Er . . . please do' said Kate.
She edged towards an upturned
pot and sat down. What else could
she do? The Tiger clearly wanted an
audience, and didn't seem about to eat
anyone – at least, not yet.

The Tiger turned down the flames
on the stove till they were a faint glow,
cleared his throat and began.

> *'All my life I've had one dream,*
> *A single goal, one constant theme,*
> *To be a chef, to wear the apron,*
> *To drizzle syrup over bacon.'*

He paused, and looked down at Kate
over his shoulder. She gulped. 'Very ni—'

'I'm talented too - in the kitchen I'm sleek!
I've perfected the rarest of pastry
  techniques.
A bain-marie? I know just what that is.
And no lacework is finer than my
  chocolate lattice.

From the lakes of Japan to the cold
  highland moors
I've served quivering jellies, pecan pies,
  s'mores . . .'

Kate looked at Rupert in a way that
meant, '*WHAT IS GOING ON?*'

Rupert stared back in a way that
meant, '*I HAVE NO IDEA BUT
AT LEAST WE'RE NOT
GETTING
EATEN?!*'

The Tiger was lost in his story.

'But where did I learn this, being born in a
    zoo?
Well, I always had grand ideas of what I
    could do.
At night I would sneak from my cage
    to the kitchen,
Made haute cuisine my single ambition!

After years of my secret, I thought,
    Take the risk!
I broke free, picked the lock with
    a rotary whisk,
Fled to the city, where I posed as
    a cook . . .
But was told time and again,
    I . . . I didn't quite "fit the look".

Upon seeing my paws, all orange
and hairy,
The screams that were screamed almost
curdled the dairy.
And so I learned that more than sharks,
unpaid debt or hairy spiders,
What people most fear are big . . .
talking . . . tigers.'

And with that the Tiger, who a mere
five minutes ago had been towering
above Kate and Roo, flopped onto a sack
of flour.

Plink.

A single tear fell from his nose.

Kate's mind was all of a jumble. If
Madame Maude wasn't lying about the

Tiger, then was she really a liar at all?
Was someone else the thief? Was it the
Tiger? And speaking of the Tiger, should
she still be scared, or did the fact that he
was crying change things somewhat?

She stopped thinking when Roo
climbed out of her pocket and crept
towards the beast.

He stretched out a snow-white paw
and patted the Tiger gently. 'There,
there,' he squeaked. 'Sometimes being a
talking animal can be tough.'

Tiger blew his nose loudly on his
apron.

'Tell me about it.'

Kate didn't point out that he'd
forgotten to rhyme. Instead, she walked

over and sat beside the Tiger too.

They stayed that way for a while, swayed by the gentle *clickety-clack* of the train and the faint rattle of spoons in the cutlery drawer.

CHAPTER TWELVE

'So,' said Tiger, who had mopped up his tears and was looking sheepishly at Kate, 'I suppose you want to know what I'm doing on this train?'

'Only if you'll talk to us in rhyme again!' said Kate with a smile.

But before he could open his mouth, a

GAAAASP!

came from the corner.

Rupert was standing next to an open cupboard, his small eyes wide at what he'd just discovered.

Gymnastics trophies. Sixteen of them.

A bundle of Ancient Scrolls.

A half-eaten packet of Extremely Flavoursome Ginger-Nut Biscuits.

Kate jumped to her feet. '*You're* the thief?' She couldn't believe what was happening. 'You've been working with Madame Maude all along!'

'*I wish!*' said Tiger. *'That woman's my GOD!*

Have you witnessed how fast she can fillet a cod?'

'So you *are* in cahoots!' exclaimed Kate. 'You've been cahooting this whole time!'

'Quite the opposite,' yawned Tiger. 'I've been trying to get her to sample my cooking and needed some extra equipment. Baking paper is just so *processed* these days. And do you really expect me to bash biscuits with anything weighing less than ten kilograms?'

There was a pause as Kate tried to

make sense of it all. 'So you stole because you want to impress Madame Maude . . . because she used to be a cook?'

'A cook? A COOK? Madame Maude did not *"used to be a cook"*! Madame Maude is behind some of the most inspired concoctions in modern cheffing! Her discoveries rival those of Anna Pavlova and the Earl of Sandwich combined!

'If I can't impress her, this journey will be my one-way trip to Exile. I've heard there is nothing to eat there but noodled eels. Nothing to remind me of the Tiger I once was.'

'But she's a . . . a . . .' stammered Kate. But what was Madame Maude? For it seemed she was no longer a thief.

'Her career was one giant lie!'

'Ah, that old walnut.' Tiger sighed. 'I suppose you heard about the whole debacle. "Clam sham", the media called it. 'All very ironic considering they weren't clams at all.'

'We know,' said Kate, exasperated. 'They were oysters! She lied to the judges about where they were from!'

'Have you ever,' said Tiger, 'stopped to think that *maybe* Madame Maude just made a mistake?'

Kate blinked. A mistake?

Tiger carried on. 'What if Madame Maude didn't lie, but simply misidentified an oyster, saying – I don't know – that it was from northern Chile, when it really originated from southern Peru?'

'And everyone ganged up on her,' said Kate quietly.

'Maybe they were waiting for her to fail,' said Rupert from the floor.

'Or maybe they were disappointed,' said Tiger gravely. 'Honestly? I really expected better of her myself. We're talking about the woman who could tell you the exact date and time – to the minute – of a cloudberry cordial from a single sniff. The woman who was so committed to the competition she tattooed a whisk on her own ankle with . . . a . . . *fork*.'

'To be fair,' said Kate, 'she doesn't help herself, not with that pointy stick and the way she bosses everyone around.'

Tiger stood up and puffed out his chest.

'Sometimes it's easier to be that way . . .' he started.

('Here we go,' muttered Rupert.)

'To poke children in corridors,
   put on a display
Of meanness and hardness and all things
   "together",
When really, inside, you feel lost as
   a feather.'

Kate was stunned. She had been wrong all this time. If what Tiger was saying was true, Madame Maude wasn't a fraud. She wasn't bad at all, not really. She had simply made a mistake.

ChApTER THIRTEEN

'I feel really bad.' Now it was Kate's turn to slump on the flour sack of sadness.

'No point in that now,' said Tiger, who was munching on the last of Simon's biscuits. 'The question is, what are you going to do about it?'

Kate sighed. There was nothing in *The Special Correspondent Manual* about this. But just as she began to head dangerously close to wallowing, a brilliant idea started to fizz in her mind.

'Quick! What's the time?'

Rupert squinted at the moon. 'Eleven twenty-one.'

'Excellent. Tiger, do you think we've got enough in the kitchen to feed everyone?'

He nodded. 'Simon's been using just eggs, which has been extremely painful to witness. There are practically mountains of ingredients here!'

Kate stood up on her flour sack. 'We are going to cook the most incredible feast RIGHT NOW! We're going to serve it for breakfast, and make Madame Maude love you.'

'And everyone else too!' piped up Rupert. 'Once they hear your story and taste your food, they'll forget all about the fact that you may have . . . er . . . "borrowed" some of their things.'

'Here's to that, my little soufflés!' said a beaming Tiger, immediately handing them each a chef's hat and apron – how he managed to procure a tiny one for Rupert, Kate would never know.

So as the train rumbled on through mountain tunnels and skated round silvery lakes, the midnight chefs began their work.

With flour on their noses and egg white clinging to their hair (and fur), they whipped up chocolate cakes, pecan pies, loaves of cherry bread, waffles, chocolate soups, quivering jellies, simmering golden sauces that they poured over sponges, and stacks and stacks of Tiger's special pancakes. He taught them how to fold pastry so it fluffed up into little birds in the oven, and how to grate chocolate so it drifted down in elegant curls.

He was an excellent teacher. Although his paws were huge and hairy, he handled each creation with delicate care.

Rupert was unexpectedly talented at

whisk-work, sitting on the handle and pedalling his legs like it was a unicycle.

'Don't let the twins see you doing that!' laughed Kate. 'They'll snap you up for the circus!'

Kate discovered she was a natural at slicing. Apricots, plums, pears – she sliced them paper thin and arranged them in flowers and zigzags on pyramids of profiteroles.

'Fabulous!' roared Tiger over the spitting sizzle of caramel. 'Pass me the apples, sous-chef Kate!'

They stopped for nothing, until every surface was covered in glittering food.

'A toast!' said Tiger. 'We must!'

And so they raised three glasses of apricot juice to the rising sun.

'To friendship!' said Rupert.

'And to not eating those friends!' said Tiger. 'Even if they would fit excellently inside an Arctic roll,' he added with a grin at Rupert, who stuck out his little pink tongue in response.

'To friendship,' echoed Kate after she stopped laughing. 'And those to come. Because I really think they'll like you as much as I do, Tiger.'

'Even Madame Maude?' he asked, his

great eyes full of longing.

'*Especially* Madame Maude. Our breakfast is going to blow her hat off.'

CHAPTER FOURTEEN

The dining car was all set up, and it
looked perfect. Rupert had even folded
the napkins into flowers.

'Gorgeous,' said Tiger. 'Now we've
only got one more thing to sort.' He
looked pointedly at Kate's dough-matted
hair and chocolate-smeared cheeks.

'You're hardly squeaky clean yourself!'
said Kate. His whiskers were all frizzed

from the steam, and there were patches of flour smudging his stripes.

'We've only got a couple of minutes,' said Rupert nervously.

'Fear not, worry-whiskers, I'll be back in less than one. Use the sink!'

Tiger whipped through the back door.

Kate ran some soapy water and was just lowering Roo into a little saucerful when she heard something creak behind her.

'Tiger? Is that you?'

'It's not,' breathed Rupert, his face even whiter than usual. 'We're toast.

Kate turned round. It was Madame Maude. Madame Maude wearing pinstriped violet and lime pyjamas. Madame Maude with the handle of a giant net clasped in her hands.

'*YOU!*'

she hissed. 'I knew it would be you! Sneaking around like I didn't know what you were up to.'

Kate gulped – she couldn't let Madame
Maude know about Tiger yet! This
wasn't how it was supposed to go at all!
No grand entrance, no charmed Madame
Maude, eager to present Tiger with a
stellar career and a Golden Whisk for his
mantelpiece.

'No, no, that's not what's going on at
all!'

'Er, yes, just think about the headlines,
Madame,' chirped Rupert. 'A . . . a
woman of a . . . er . . . certain *age*, with
experience in the most disciplined of
culinary environments, collides with a
headstrong child –'

'How do you know about that?'
Madame Maude snapped. 'About my
work.'

'The Golden Whisk?' Kate ventured. 'We . . . we recognised you from the papers!'

'Nonsense!' Madame Maude spoke in a voice so low Kate could barely hear it, but which made it all the more terrifying.

'You weren't even born then, you lying little sneak. You know what I think? I think you've been creeping around in everyone's compartments, rifling through their *private* things with your jammy little fingers and taking whatever you fancy! Whipping up a frenzy about some non-existent tiger to help you out! I mean . . . What. A. Ridiculous. LIE! A tiger? On a train?!'

'That's what we thought about *you*,'

Kate argued back. 'But it turns out we were totally wrong! You're no villain! You just have to believe that *I'm* not either.'

'Then indulge me,' demanded Madame Maude. 'If it's not you two, then who's the real thief?'

Kate didn't know what to say. Should she tell Madame Maude about Tiger? But there was no way she would believe it – not without hearing his story first.

But she needn't have worried.

'Madame Maude,' said Tiger, stepping out of the shadows and extending a shaking paw, '*enchanté*. I'm a *huge* fan.'

CHAPTER FIFTEEN

Madame Maude went as white as a
white tablecloth. Then whiter still.
'Has he killed her with words?'
whispered Rupert.
Then came the spluttering.
If Kate hadn't known how
unvillainous Madame Maude
really was, she would have

found it quite satisfying. All right, maybe
a bit of her still did.

'I don't want to eat you,' Tiger said
wearily to Madame Maude, and Kate
realised just how many times he must
have had to say that over the years.
'I want to . . . well . . . I want to eat
breakfast *with* you. The breakfast I made.'

Madame Maude stopped spluttering
and eyed him up and down.
'What?'

'I've been a follower
of yours since the very
beginning!' Tiger
exclaimed. '*How to
Cook Well for People
You Don't Like* was

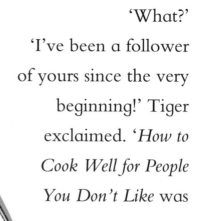

my bread and butter all those years in the zoo!'

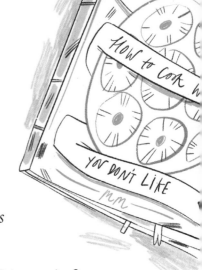

'You . . . you taught yourself from scratch?' Madame Maude sniffed. 'From that *baseless* book?'

'I agree – *A Matter of Distaste* is far superior. But indeed I did. And I was distraught when you were barred from your position.'

'Don't be,' she sighed. 'Only a fool would confuse oysters from such vastly different regions.'

'I thought northern Chile and southern Peru were neighbours,' muttered Kate to Rupert.

'You're no fraud, Madame Maude,' said Tiger. 'You're an inspiration – the very reason I've chosen this culinary life. And I've always kept a poster of you tucked under my pillow – your pointy stick and sour expression always spurred me on. Would you perhaps –' Tiger bowed low and extended a paw once more – 'join me for breakfast?'

Kate had never heard him sound so earnest.

'I will,' said Madame Maude in a voice that seemed to have thawed a few degrees. She took his paw in her bony hand.

Kate smiled and followed them into the dining car with Rupert in her pocket. *What* a story!

CHAPTER SIXTEEN

The passengers woke that morning to a muddle of delicious smells. What was that? Pastries? Hot coffee? Pear and mascarpone tarts with a warm raspberry compote?!

Doors opened into corridors, where, clad in dressing gowns and nightcaps, befuddled passengers rubbed sleep from their eyes and began to make their way up the train. When they reached the dining car, they found it transformed.

'Kate?' Dad was blinking in confusion. 'What's going on?'

'Just sit down, Dad,' said Kate with a smile. 'We'll explain everything after breakfast.'

'Who's *we*?'

'Me,' said Madame Maude, still in her pinstriped pyjamas, sidling up beside Kate with an enormous plate of crispy bacon balanced on her palm.

Dad's eyes widened and he flopped down into a seat next to the Russian priest, speechless.

'Have you tried this, Kate's dad?' The priest waggled a croissant the size of a small pillow under Dad's nose. 'Second only to my holy wafers!'

What a feast it was.

'This is genius!' said the twins together, as they marvelled at pastry swans floating in a pond of raspberry juice.

'I have never tasted anything like this in my short, sweet life,' mumbled Simon through mouthfuls of cinnamon toast.

'And I raise my juice to whoever whipped this cream!' declared Miss Bonbon. 'I cannot imagine the finesse it must have taken!'

From his little picnic spread on

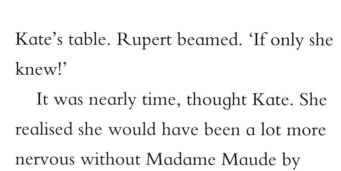

Kate's table. Rupert beamed. 'If only she knew!'

It was nearly time, thought Kate. She realised she would have been a lot more nervous without Madame Maude by her side.

Kate climbed up onto a table and cleared her throat. With clinks and murmurs, quiet settled.

'Everyone,' she began,

Whoop!

'I think we can all agree on something: this breakfast has been one of the best we've ever had.'

'Hear, hear!' said the twins in funny voices.

'And I'd very much like to introduce you to the genius behind it all. Come out, Tiger!'

Tiger stepped out from the kitchen and into full view. His chef's hat was on his head and his apron was tied around his waist. He looked magnificent.

Silence fell like snow.

And then there was a single clap. And then another. Dad stood up, the twins started wolf-whistling, the priest whooped. Madame Maude cheered and the whole dining car erupted into applause.

'I don't even care if he wants to eat me!' yelled Simon. 'I'll die happy and full!'

Once everything had settled down, Tiger was the centre of attention.

He explained the whole story, and even brought out Miss Bonbon's trophies with a sorry face.

'I'm *profoundly* sorry,' he said. 'I simply couldn't find anything in the kitchen up to the job of mashing things.

'If I'm honest, I quite like the idea that even my trophies are as talented as I am,' she replied.

'And here –' he presented Simon with an enormous platter of home-made ginger-nut biscuits – 'these are for you.'

ChAPTER SEVENTEEN

The train was rumbling towards its final
stop. Looking through the steamed-up
windows at the whiteness outside, Kate
thought it must be the only colour for

miles, until she saw a little pink station in the distance. As they got closer, she could make out a figure on the platform, wearing a very vivid snowsuit and looking every part the explorer. Mum.

Kate leaped off the train as soon as it chugged to a halt and ran straight into Mum's arms, with no thought for her luggage or the fact that her hat had fallen off.

THE ARCTIC

Soon Dad was wrapping them both in a huge hug.

'I've missed you so much,' said Mum, her voice muffled by the tightness of the hug. 'I can't believe you've come all this way!'

'I wouldn't be anywhere else in the world,' said Kate.

It turned out that Mum had made her big discovery just a few hours before, and the famous newspaper *The Lookout Post* was helicoptering in a reporter to get the scoop on the secrets Arctic seaweed had apparently been keeping for millennia.

'Speaking of Special Correspondents, I've got a feeling my favourite one is harbouring a story.' She winked at Kate.

'Well,' said Kate, 'I think I'm going to need some help telling you.'

She looked behind her and motioned to Tiger, who was waiting in the doorway. He stepped off the train, one of Madame Maude's scarves flapping elegantly behind him.

Mum didn't even blink. She walked up

to Tiger and embraced what she could reach of him, before saying, 'You know what, the story can wait for now. I'm starving. Did anyone remember to bring me some food?'

Dear Kate,

I read your article in *The Lookout Post*. Congratulations — it was an excellent read. I am so glad Madame Maude wasn't the villain you thought she was. It shows real guts to say when you're wrong, and report on it too.

Please find enclosed a proposal. I would very much value your help, if you could spare it.

Yours sincerely,

Catherine Rodriguez

The END

Look out for more Special Correspondent Adventures from Kate & Rupert

COMING SOON!

PRESS

Thank you for choosing a Piccadilly Press book.

If you would like to know more about our authors, our books or if you'd just like to know what we're up to, you can find us online.

www.piccadillypress.co.uk

And you can also find us on:

We hope to see you soon!